Snow Bunny's Christmas Wish

To Sharon, because you're a star!

Lots of love, Bek xxx

First published in 2012 by Nosy Crow Ltd

The Crow's Nest, 10a Lant Street

London SE1 1QR

www.nosycrow.com

ISBN 978 0 85763 179 4

Nosy Crow and associated logos are trademark

and/or registered trademarks of Nosy Crow Ltd.

A CIP catalogue record for this book is available from the British Library.

Printed in China

10 9 8 7 6 5 4 3 2 1

Snow Bunny's Christmas Wish

Rebecca Harry

nosy crow

Snow Bunny lived all by herself
deep in the wintry forest.

Every day she hummed a happy song,
but there was one thing she wished
for more than anything.

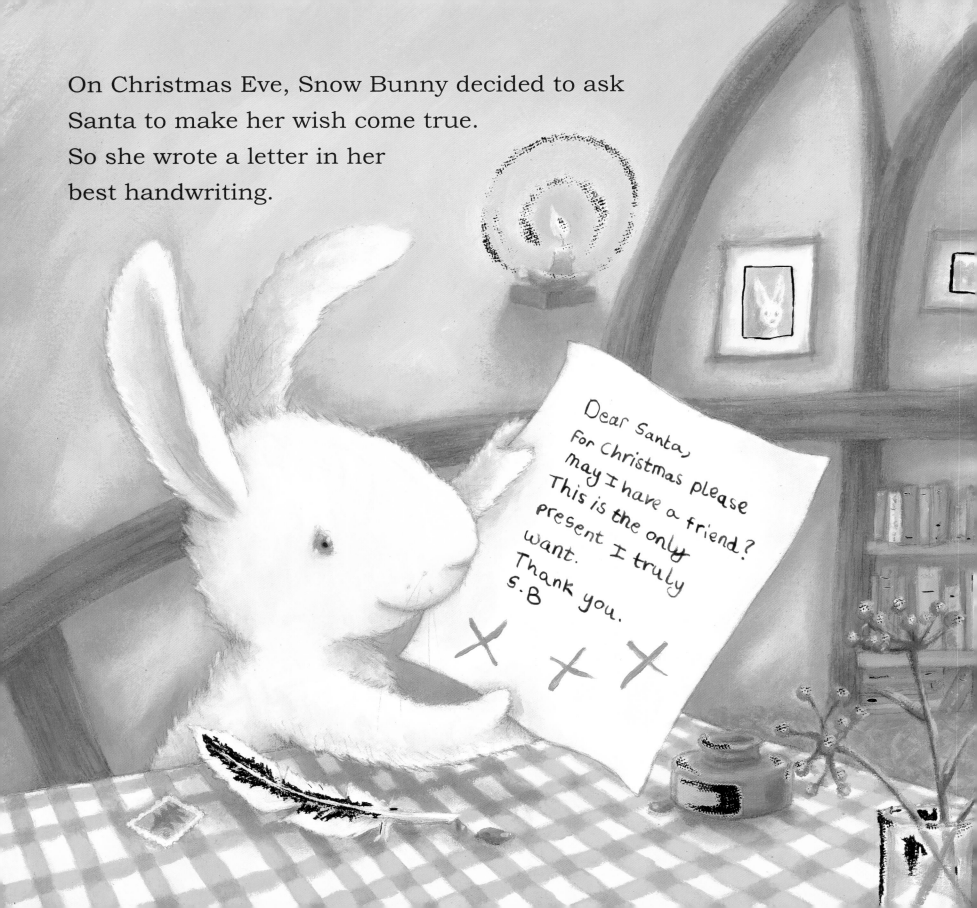

On Christmas Eve, Snow Bunny decided to ask
Santa to make her wish come true.
So she wrote a letter in her
best handwriting.

Dear Santa,
For Christmas please
may I have a friend?
This is the only
present I truly
want.
Thank you.
S.B
X X X

She addressed
the envelope carefully so it
wouldn't get lost in the post,

and she hurried out
into the frosty air just in time . . .

. . . to see Red Robin Postman flying away.
She had missed the post by a whisker.

"Oh, no!" said Snow Bunny. "I shall have
to deliver my letter to Santa myself."

Snow Bunny looked at her map.

"I will follow the North Star to Santa's house," she said. "I won't get lost, but just in case, I'd better pack some useful things."

North Star

Wintry Forest

Frozen Pond

She packed a pair of warm
mittens . . .

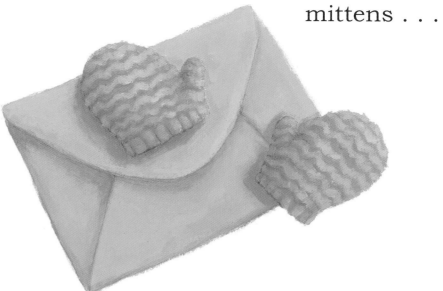

. . . some iced biscuits

. . . and her map.

Snow Bunny had been tramping
through the snow for a little while when
she saw a light shimmering through the trees.

"There's the North Star!"
she said happily.
But as she pushed through the trees, she saw . . .

. . . it was only the moon shining on a frozen pond.
Bears skated across the ice, all having fun . . .

. . . except one small cub,

who sat by himself
blowing on his cold,
cold paws.

Snow Bunny thought for a moment.
"You can have my mittens to keep
your paws warm," she said kindly,
and she went on her way.

She hadn't gone far
when she spotted a
star high above the trees.

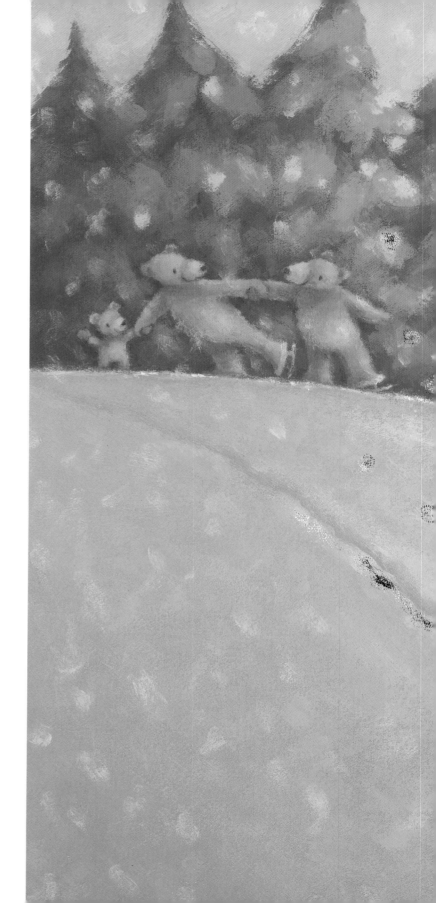

"That must be the North Star!"
she said hopefully.
But as she came down the hill, she saw. . .

. . . it was the star on top of a huge Christmas tree.

Animals scampered around, hanging decorations from its pretty branches – all except one little fox cub, who had no decoration to add.

Snow Bunny thought for a moment.
"You can use my iced biscuits to
decorate the tree," she said
kindly to the fox cub . . .

. . . and she went on her way.

She had gone quite far when she saw a wavering light.
"Is that the North Star?" she wondered, but on the
other side of the hedge, she saw . . .

. . . the light shone from the lanterns of some fawns, who had been out visiting and had lost their way.

Snow Bunny thought for
a moment.

"You can have my map so you can find
the path home," she said kindly.
And they went on their way.

Snow Bunny blew on her cold paws.
She felt hungry and a little bit lost.

Then she took one last
long look up at the sky, and
what did she see?

"That *must* be the North Star!" she
exclaimed. "It is so big and beautiful!"
And as she ran towards it she saw . . .

. . . that it *was* the North Star, shining brightly over Santa's house!

Santa read Snow Bunny's letter.
"Hop on my sleigh. I'll drop you home
on my way delivering presents
and making wishes come true
around the world."

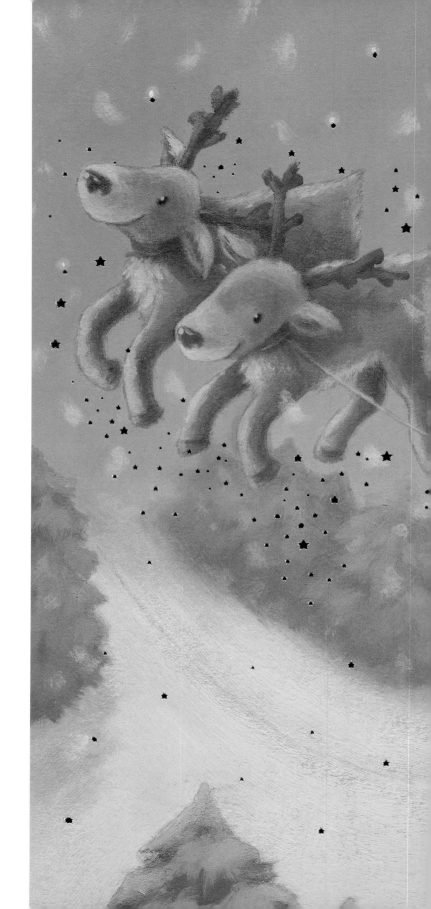

"But what about my wish, Santa?"
Snow Bunny asked politely.

"Wait and see," smiled Santa, and with a "giddy-up",
they whooshed off through the dark and starry night.

As Santa's sleigh landed outside her home deep in the wintry forest, Snow Bunny saw all the animals she'd met along the way gathered at her door.

They had all come to
thank Snow Bunny for her help.

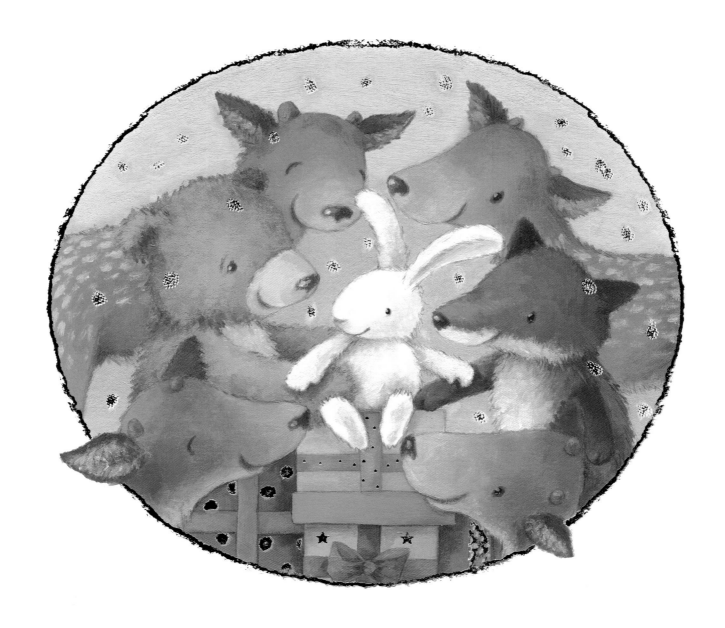

What a happy Christmas the new
best friends spent together!
Snow Bunny's Christmas
wish had come true.